PRAISE FOR DAN BERNITT

Yelling at Bananas in Whole Foods

"By the time we get to the moment described in the title, Dan Bernitt's piece has taken us on a journey deep into the rabbit hole of self-obsession. The Brooklyn-based storyteller and playwright recounts a year in which his obsessions got the best of him, leaving him isolated and emotionally unstable. It all came down to food, as a chance meeting with a '90s-era motivational speaker drove him to be a vegetarian, then a vegan, and finally a raw-food enthusiast. Bernitt is merciless with his grad-school self, who cuts himself off from the outside world by being a real jerk about healthy eating. When the breakdown finally comes, it's harsh and funny and unforgettably absurd."

– MINNEAPOLIS *CITY PAGES*

"★★★★½ — In his latest monologue, Bernitt, one of the most fully engaging performers you'll see at the Fringe, details his journey from a desolate New Mexico artist colony to a public breakdown in a New York City Whole Foods. While some of his life experiences are more unusual than most and make for a great story in and of themselves, it's Bernitt's ability to fantastically describe ordinary details that take his writing a step above most. He could easily leave behind the world of theatre and follow in the footsteps of David Sedaris or Augusten Burroughs. And like those authors, he isn't afraid to share the details that make him look less favorable, including the aftermath of a one-night stand gone wrong and phone call confessionals with his mother."

– INDIANAPOLIS *NUVO*

Phi Alpha Gamma

"MUST-SEE SHOW ... The fast-paced piece examines masculinity, faith, brotherhood, and love in a college fraternity struggling to deal with two brothers, one an imprisoned gay-basher and the other newly emerged from the closet. Bernitt's savvy script offers few easy answers and plenty of twists that toy with the audience's sympathies."

– ST. PAUL *PIONEER PRESS*

"Only in his early twenties ... Bernitt's solo piece, *Phi Alpha Gamma*, moved, surprised, and even shocked some Fringegoers. Its harsh portrayal on homophobia and its emotional residue in a college fraternity understands the tragic psychology of homophobia. Hence, it's rendered with anguish, not vindictiveness. ... He's an exciting young writer-performer." – *LAVENDER MAGAZINE*

"Dan Bernitt's one-man show about how a college fraternity attempts to deal with homophobia after an incident in which one of its members is convicted of violently assaulting a gay man is a complex, intricately structured piece of performance art. He manages, through the skillful evocation of several different characters, to dissect the menacing dynamics lurking beneath the fraternity's socially-responsible public face. But he also puts us in the place of the imprisoned attacker, now a victim himself. The combination of dramatic anthropology and revenge fantasy is intense and skillfully observed."

Thanks for the Scabies, Jerkface!

"Bernitt navigates the changing moods of his work with easy confidence and charming wit. He keeps the audience rooting for him in the tales of his misadventures. ... One of America's next great monologists."

"Bernitt re-enacts his essay-like monologues in a casual storytelling style, offering oblique insights as he details some of the most uncomfortable moments of his young life. ... Bernitt's charming quips and burgeoning potential prove, well, contagious."

YELLING AT BANANAS IN WHOLE FOODS

❧

YELLING AT BANANAS IN WHOLE FOODS

†

DAN BERNITT

SAWYER HOUSE
2015

SAWYER HOUSE

FIRST EDITION, September 2015.

Publisher's Cataloging-in-Publication Data
Bernitt, Dan (1986–).
    Yelling at bananas in whole foods / by Dan Bernitt. —1ST ed.
    p. cm.
    ISBN-13: 978-0-9821560-5-6
    ISBN-10: 0-9821560-5-7
    I. Title.

Library of Congress Control Number: 2013917687

Cover photograph © 2012 by Dan Bernitt.

www.sawyerhouse.net

for you

Performance History

Yelling at Bananas in Whole Foods was commissioned in 2012 by The Berkshire Fringe (artistic directors Sara Katzoff, Timothy Ryan Olson, Peter Wise). Its first performance was on July 26, 2012, at the Daniel Arts Center on the campus of Bard College at Simon's Rock in Great Barrington, Massachusetts. It was directed by Paul Takacs.

The version reflected in this book was first performed on August 2, 2013, at the New Century Theatre in Minneapolis, Minnesota, as part of the Minnesota Fringe Festival.

This Is Stonewall was part of *The Gayer Show*, a duo performance with Les Kurkendaal. Its first performance was on May 30, 2009, at Below Zero Lounge in Cincinnati, Ohio, as part of the Cincinnati Fringe Festival.

Ghoti was first performed on June 26, 2014, at Newlin Hall in Centre College's Norton Center for the Arts in Danville, Kentucky, for the Kentucky Governor's School for the Arts.

Contents

Boy and His Shirt

I'M NOT SURE WHY I WATCHED IT, BUT the other day I watched a TED Talk about aging. A psychologist named Dan Gilbert wanted to study why people make decisions that our future selves will later regret. He found that we fundamentally misunderstand time; as a result, our likes, dislikes, values, personality—these all change over time far more than we anticipate. With one striking graph, he showed that an eighteen-year-old thinks she'll change as much as a 50-year-old *actually does.*[1]

The night before I turned 24 I sat in my casita in Taos, New Mexico, drinking plenty of Santa Fe Pale Ale, and a fit of nostalgia had me clicking through old photographs of myself. There was a photograph of me at seventeen, another one of me taken less than a year prior, and as I sat there, I realized I was wearing the same black T-shirt. This shirt had been with me for seven years.

I looked at the boy, and I looked at the young man. They looked like different people. Hair loss and facial hair growth have that effect.

---

1 I don't want to lose you on the first page of this book, but if you want to see more from Dan Gilbert's talk, it's available here: http://www.ted.com/talks/dan_gilbert_you_are_always_changing. (I'll be waiting for you back at the second paragraph.)

This photograph was taken in August 2003, and Dan, a senior in high school, performed a gig at the Beaumont Center YMCA in Lexington, Kentucky.

This Dan wants to be a folksinger. At this point in his life he's recorded in his bedroom two music albums, and he's figuring out how to entertain people at open mics around town. He dreams of having a life (and dreadlocks!) like his hero, Ani DiFranco. The message ironed on his T-shirt says "Not in Our Name: A Statement of Conscience," a petition he signed in protest of the Iraq War. And for some reason he's wearing a candy necklace. Four months later he will discover that he can grow a full beard. (He hasn't owned a razor since.)

There's something about this photograph, stretched out more than its pixels permit, that shows off the sparkle in this boy's eyes. He's eager. He's on the verge of something. He yearns. His smiles still show off his teeth.

This was before he ever performed outside of his hometown. This was before he ever drove outside Lexington by himself. This was when his world was just beginning to open, and he thought he was unstoppable. This boy thought a guitar would never leave his side. You dream a lot of things at 17.

In the six years between the previous photograph and this one, he's relied on equal parts audacity and support. This young man has written three solo performances, published two books of plays, performed in fifteen theater festivals, received support from several generous funders, and submitted his passport application to the State Department one week before his first performance outside the country. No wonder his hair is starting to thin.

The T-shirt is the same, save the destruction of the iron-on paper. The ends survived, but the middle section has, um, changed. Damned washing machines, washing away that which isn't strong enough to stay.

The calluses once on his fingertips have moved to different parts of the body. The first review of his work patronized him: "The most glorious thing about being so young is that you think you're the first to think big thoughts." The next day another review encouraged him to keep going. Ego, narcissism, those funny and fragile things.

It took this young man a long time to shut up and listen. It took plenty of exposure to begin to react without defensiveness. Eventually he realized,

Full Scalp: dreams of dreadlocks
Contact Lenses: never take them out
Shiny Skin: overworked oil gla
Septoplasty: to fix chronic sinus infections, often resulting in laryngitis
Clean Cut: 'I'm harmless'
Candy Necklace: what were you thinking?
Political Slogan T-Shirt: how fashionable to stand for something

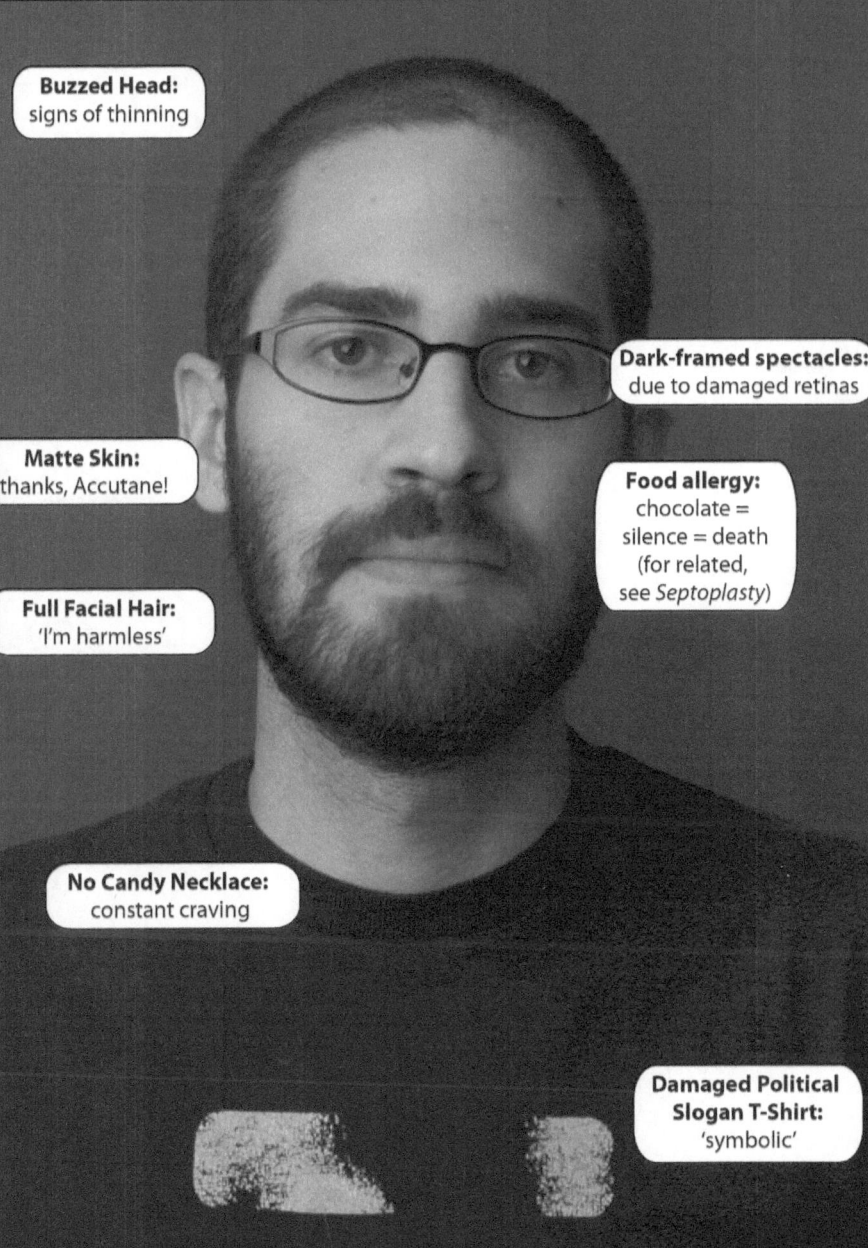

"I'm not writing for everybody; I'm writing for you."

Yelling at Bananas in Whole Foods

Officer, look, I'm very sorry. I came back here because I wanted to apologize and explain myself. Officer, I've been thinking a lot about this on the way over. This might make you laugh; it might piss you off. I don't know. How you react is up to you. This is all really hard to explain, but I trust you'll listen. I'll get somewhere with this.

Before I went to Taos, New Mexico, for a three-month retreat at an artist residency—I was there to write plays for three months—my father told me to take lots of pictures of the beautiful landscape. He'd regularly tell me, "If you don't have a picture, it didn't happen."

I don't like photos; I'd rather let people use their imagination.

Here's Taos!

Isn't it beautiful? Doesn't everything look better with an Instagram filter?

DAN BERNITT

This is a screenshot from my iPhone. Yep, that's what Grindr looks like. If you don't know, Grindr is an app that allows gay men to see how many feet away the nearest gay male is. I'm used to people being less than 180 feet away; I'm from New York. But here in Taos? The nearest gay male is back in Santa Fe: 52.7 miles away. This'll be a lonely three months.

When you're in the middle of nowhere without a car (because you're too young to rent one, so you have no way of getting around or escaping), you'll need some handy boundaries for when you're walking. This is the Guadalajara Grille. There's one to the north and another to the south. There is nothing cool you can walk to past either point. If you find yourself at a Grille, *get the fish tacos*. They're amazing.

This is a dog. He's been abandoned. I've named him "Nuts." (You can see he hasn't been neutered.) When you walk around Taos, you're bound to see several dogs either walking alone or in small packs. Because there's nothing else to do here, you may spend some nights following them around. Caution: do not get attached, even if Nuts starts following *you*. Also, don't bother feeding Nuts canned tuna; he's not interested.

This is a tree where vultures live. It's above where I live. Several blocks of sidewalk underneath are covered in splatters of black and white vulture feces. When I first saw it, I wondered, "why does the desert have a Jackson Pollock mural?"

DAN BERNITT

This is a dead bird. It's starting to decompose on my doorstep. One afternoon I heard a single knock at my front door. I was so excited, because I thought someone wanted to say hello. Nope. This bird had just flown to its death.

And this is the inside of my casita, where I spend nearly all my time. Alone.

DAN BERNITT

By the third week I've gotten pretty bored with myself. I spend a lot of my time sitting on the floor – the ceilings are very low, and I'm too tall to stand up straight – so I sit on the floor, eat leftover tuna out of a can, and listen to Prince's entire discography. This is not what I imagined the life of an artist to be. What isolates me even more: of the ten artists here, I'm the only guy and the only one under the age of fifty. I have nothing against women in their fifties, but when I hang out with them, they talk to me like I'm their son, not their equal. Or they talk at length about the gingko biloba and chlorophyll supplements they're taking.

I do spend a lot of time talking to another woman who's in her fifties: my mother. I call my mom a lot.

"Well, if you're having a rough time out there, maybe you could find a church," she says.

This is not the time to tell my mother I'm an atheist. I tell her, "Mom, it's a weird conflict. I came here to write. I'm here to write plays. I thought I'd wake up in the morning, feeling refreshed by the desert. I'd see tumbleweeds or sage bushes and think, 'this is inspiring!' But it's not working like that. Everything depresses me:

dead birds, abandoned dogs, vulture shit. I don't want to go outside, but I don't wanna stay in. I'm tired of eating, but I don't wanna starve. I'm drinking so much it's not fun anymore. And I don't wanna write either because the play I'm working on is about AIDS, and it's really starting to scare me, but I have to be productive and work on my thesis for my MFA. I mean, I'm glad to have a break from grad school, but I need structure, something stimulating, something that's not me 24/7. Mom, I've jerked off so much even *that* is boring."

The whole time I'm saying this, there's an echo on the line. Everything I say comes back to me and sounds more pitiful than I intended.

"Ew!" My mother answers. "Okay. That's bad. Um. How about – how about you take that camera Dad and I got ya, and, y'know, you could take some pictures of some food at some restaurants. If you ask nicely, maybe you could get some recipes together. You could make a cookbook!"

"'Make a cookbook'?"

"Yeah! Or something! A fun, little project!"

"That's a great solution for a different problem, Mom. I've thought about leaving, but so many people apply to have three months to write, and so

DAN BERNITT

many people don't get that opportunity. I've never felt this before, I've never felt something I cannot convey in words. I can't leave. Thanks for letting me vent, Mom. Bye."

When I hang up on my mother, I realize few people will understand what this is like. Dear Self: Stop complaining. So I resolve to spend the remainder of my three months making do – with kamikaze birds being the only guests who knock on my door. I thought I'd be thrilled to be here, but –

This is how I feel.

• • •

The next afternoon I've had enough of this artist life. I'm at a coffeeshop, Googling "cheapest way to escape Taos," while a middle-aged, punky lesbian makes me a mango smoothie.

It's about a thousand dollars to fly out of here, but there's always a $200 Greyhound. Am I seriously considering taking two suitcases across the desert on a two-day bus ride with two transfers from Albuquerque back to Port Authority? Maybe.

The woman sets my drink in front of me: "Cheer up – here's the best mango smoothie in all of Taos." She smiles, the friendliest anyone has been to me in town, and I feel a connection to this woman. Have we met before?

Suddenly some kid outside starts screaming in a horrifyingly primal way. I look out at this child and think, "there's my spirit animal." The father screams at his son: "You are not! – going! – to behave like this!" It only ignites more fury in the boy. The father and son continue yelling back and forth at each other, until the father picks up his son by his T-shirt and carries him out of Taos Plaza like a gym bag.

The barista froths milk as she looks outside. "He's screwed. The parents are screwed, *and* the young boy is screwed. He's crying, he's sad about something, let him cry. You tell him, 'I will speak to you when you learn to speak in a proper tone.' *That* is what you say. You do not yell. What that father just taught a three-year-old is that it's okay to scream your head off — and that *that's* okay. You know what he's gonna grow up to be? Listen. He's going to be a mass murderer. And they were a lovely family."

She keeps talking about how best to raise children, and my mind nags me: I *have* met this woman before. The more I think, the more I feel she was part of *my* childhood. I hear her voice, and I can feel the texture of a pilled fabric sofa I'd sit on as a kid as I watched TV. Was she on TV? What show was it?

"Hello-o-o? Do you have a name?" She waves her arms in front of me.

"Sorry. I'm Dan."

"How's your smoothie, Dan? That's good."

And then – she winks.

It's that wink!

When I was seven, I taped a show she was on, and I would rewind her wink and watch it again and again because it looked so sassy! And I got in such trouble, too, because I taped over the final episode of "Dynasty." My mother was livid. She screamed at me, but later I would sit in my room and memorize the infomercial I finally had on tape. "Ahhh! Stop the insanity!" The words jump into the present from the 1990s. "She lost 133 pounds, but she didn't go from being a fat person to a thin person, that's not what happened, she went from being an unfit person to a fit person, and *so can you*!"

"Oh, my God. Are you Susan Powter? Are you the lady who talks to fat people, but you don't talk to fat people, you really don't, you speak to anybody who can't walk up a flight of stairs without sucking wind, two stairs kill ya, doesn't matter if you're a size two? You are Susan Powter, right? *OMIGAWD*."

She looks at me with a bit of shock—because I'm quoting her infomercial to her. The infomercial that made her millions of dollars, but somehow she's now in a coffeeshop? Well, she laughs (thank God) and winks at me again.

"What are you doing in New Mexico?! I wanna ask you all the questions – who what where when why and *how*?! You were on TV all the time, and then you disappeared."

"First, set the record straight: I did not 'disappear.' For obvious reasons: I'm still here. Ta-da. No, I fired everybody and moved to an island off the coast of Seattle because I was tired of having lawyers around me all the time. I'm a big moneymaker, did you hear that? But I'm back, baby! I am enraged, I am volcanic! That's why I came back to work. Dan, lemme ask you something—"

Guys! Susan Powter is talking to *me*. In real life.

"Now I don't say this to everyone, because it'd be bad for business, and I love the people I work for. I only tell you this because you look smart; you are smart, right? Have you ever juiced a carrot? I'm serious. Have you ever juiced a carrot? Let's say you juice a carrot. Let's say you juice thirty carrots. You cannot physically eat thirty carrots, but you can juice them. You'll get all sorts of vitamins and nutrients, but you'll also get a lot of other things in your glass. Do you know how many pesticides are on thirty carrots? Dan, the same goes for mangoes.

"Oh, stop making that face, you'll be fine; I try to tell people these things, but they'll immediately put their hand up. They don't want to hear it. They'll say to me, 'Susan, I don't want to hear it, because I am quite happy with how I live my life.'

And that's fine. If you *want* to live your life laying down for The Man every day, you go right ahead and do it, because he will leave you without nothin', money, health, nothin'. But what do you have if you don't have your health?"

Customers walk into the shop, and Susan assumes the barista position.

"Intentional and conscious, Dan. Those are the two words for living a decent life. I can't believe you don't know about this, but, *ha!*, believe me, you can be smart and still not know things. You have Netflix on that computer, right? Look up *Food, Inc.* You'll love it. You'll watch it, watch it right now, we'll talk later. Consider it a class, Sister Brother. The Politics of Stupid 101." Then she turns to a customer and says, "Welcome. What can I get you?"

• • •

An hour and a half later I storm out of the coffeeshop, muttering, "What is happening in the world?!"

I immediately call my mother.

When she picks up, she doesn't say hello. She greets me with "so, when are you leaving?"

"Oh, no, I ain't leaving! Mom. Do you remember infomercials?! Well, there was this one where this woman would scream 'Stop the Insanity.' Her name was Susan Powter. She was this motivational speaker, she had this platinum-blonde flat-top haircut, eyes like slits, and she was, like, super aggressive when she'd talk. She had this weight loss infomercial, and she'd say stuff like 'eat potatoes, don't eat steak, just eat seven potatoes!'"

"Yeah... She was on really late at night, right? Gosh golly, she was annoying."

"*I just met her at a coffeeshop, Mom!*"

"Oh, that's interesting. What brings her to town?"

"She's *working* at the coffeeshop! I don't know what happened, something about lawyers, Seattle, but that's not the point. Mom, I gave her my phone number, and I got her email address, and we're gonna hang out! I'm gonna hang out with Susan Powter! And she's gonna teach me about how scary the food industry is! She has so many stories, Mom! She said to me as I left, 'I have stories like you wouldn't believe!' I believe it!"

"Daniel... Is this a good decision? I mean, are you sure you want to know all that stuff? I took a class once where we read 'The Jungle,' and there's a part about workers getting ground up along with the beef – phew, took me a while to eat meat again."

"*Yeah!* Isn't that exciting?! I mean, that's gross, but... Mom, I've never considered what to eat or where my food comes from! I feel like I'm learning how to eat!!"

"Baby, you already know how to eat. Do you need me to send you some recipes?"

"No. That's not what I mean. I'm calling because I'm *excited* about something... I feel like I have a friend here."

Walking down to the Guadalajara Grille, Taos has a whole new shimmer to it. Even the abandoned dogs are beautiful, how they all appear to trot with a purpose. I'm walking with purpose now, too— no longer aimless and bored.

At the Guadalajara Grille, I place an order for three fish tacos with pico de gallo and sour cream, a side of rice and pinto beans, and a cold Fresca sold in a glass bottle. On a rack beside the counter is a stack of newspapers. And I see one headline: "Oil continues to spill into Gulf." (This was in 2010.)

An oil rig exploded and killed eleven people, and now millions of barrels of oil are gushing into the Gulf of Mexico. The oil is still flowing. Efforts are being made to cap the spill, but it may take weeks to do so — and clean-up will take much longer.

I think back to third grade, when my family lived in Key West. Our house backed up to the Gulf of Mexico. My science teacher, Mrs. Setchell, taught us about the oceans, how there may be many of them, but it's really one ocean. If more oil flows into the Gulf, it may flow into the Atlantic and beyond. What's gonna happen to sea life, estuaries, the fishing industry? All these could be contaminated. Destroyed. In my mind, I see images of manatees and pelicans covered in oil, dolphins who have to swim through oil to reach the surface for air...

I don't know if anyone knows right now how far or wide this spill is going to go.

The server brings my fish tacos. I think about *Food, Inc.* I think about the oil spill.

This will be my last meal with meat.

I eat slow and enjoy every bite, but when I finish, I see others eat around me. Each bite brings them closer and closer to a spill that will slowly seep its way into their dinners.

• • •

"I said 'Stop the Insanity' over 150 years ago, but which insanity would you like to talk about?"

This is a week later. Susan Powter records herself talking to her computer. I sit across from her.

Between us: a one-terabyte external hard drive. Let the friendship begin!

"You wanted to talk about food, let's talk about food. There are two types of people in this world, Dan: the people who are going to hear what I have to say and only hear words, and then there are the people who will *listen* to what I say and truly get it. If you are living in a human body, your body needs food. I don't know any human body that doesn't. But these days you have to prepare to go about your day as if you are living in war. There's bovine growth hormone, antibiotics, food is picked from trees and ripened with gas, it's a Holocaust of apples, it's true, it's true; so if you are eating anything but organic, you might as well lay down and die. You wanna know the five rules of food? First rule: if it glows in the dark, we don't eat it. If it's fluorescent, I suggest you get rid of it! Number two, if I go to buy tomato sauce and I don't see the word 'tomato' anywhere on the ingredient list, I'm not putting it in my body."

She never finishes the five rules. She leaves me hanging at number two. But she speaks with such enthusiasm I can't help but stay on for the ride. Not only does she know everything about food and nutrition, but also she becomes an encyclopedia of feminist thought when she starts mixing in quotes from everyone ranging from Emma Goldman to Gertrude Stein to Audre Lorde to—wait, did she just quote Paris Hilton?

"What do I mean by that, what do I mean about anything, what I mean by that is — Grains! Beans! Fruits! Vegetables! Eighty percent of your diet should consist of these whole, real, organic foods. What can I get you?"

The coffeeshop is still open! She fascinates me to no end. But I want to talk *with* her – you know, like a friend. After we talk, I hope that maybe she'll invite me to her house to cook. Or maybe she could teach me yoga. We could make a cookbook! I want to bring up all these ideas, but she never pauses.

"Haveagoodnightwherewerewe." The lecture continues on and on. At some point I can't tell if I'm getting tired or if she's actually speaking nonsense, but I swear I hear something like, "why aren't my eyes ever blended hi-fi lo-fi squirrel brisket I know it's totally indie from the nineties *hahahaha* don't you get it?"

"Yeah. I get everything." Even when she says things that are absurd, it all sounds inspiring.

I don't know how much time passes, but she finishes her lecture because the one-terabyte hard drive is full. I am exhausted from sitting there, my brain full from this boot camp.

I get up from my seat, and she hugs me goodbye. It's a warm embrace. I haven't hugged anyone in months. "See ya later, Dan." As I walk back to the artist colony, bits of the stream-of-consciousness conversation begin to click in my head: Find out what foods make you feel great. Be careful eating things from a factory. Don't be a human sacrifice to Nabisco!

My pantry features cereal, frozen waffles, microwaveable dinners, a case of Santa Fe Pale Ale... It finally makes sense: the most political thing I can do is control what I put in my body.

I grab the pack of stale glazed donuts and walk outside. With a donut in my grip, I wind up like an Olympian and toss it into the desert: "I don't need this shit anymore! I will be healthy!" Suddenly I see two dogs run into the desert, competing with each other on who will eat the donuts the fastest. They're barking and playing under the moonlight, gobbling up what I toss out. There are a few things I might miss about New Mexico.

• • •

I fly back to New York for my final year of grad school. In the mornings when I walk to class, I listen to Susan Powter podcasts as I admire the gentlemen now within reach, the eye candy of lower Manhattan. I strut along 9th Street with a canvas bag full of grains, beans, fruits, and vegetables.

During the middle of class, we take a break for lunch. The other playwrights go to pick up fast food. It's not that I judge them—okay, maybe I do—but I feel bad when I see them eat food that doesn't make them glow. One guy eats sesame chicken over fried rice with an egg roll, washes it down with a 20-ounce soda, and says twenty minutes later, "Ugh! Why do I always feel tired after lunch? I ha-a-ate this."

That's a fair question. Now I know the science behind it, but I don't wanna get too detailed.

"Well, you're having a sugar crash," I say. "You could prevent that by eating lighter stuff, like fruits, vegetables, quinoa... You know, ever since I became a vegetarian —"

Without any specific prompting, I start to talk about the greatness of how I eat, how much better I feel when I eat celery, hummus, field greens and tomatoes, Brussels sprouts roasted in olive oil salt pepper, throw those in the oven, twenty, thirty minutes, 375 degrees, *the flavor is divinity!*

Our instructor interrupts my litany of delicious dishes and recipes: "Just don't turn into some vegan. Maybe it's the lack of protein, but not a single vegan I know has a sense of humor."

Everyone lets out a guffaw. Then class continues with yet another discussion of *Oedipus Rex*—for the seventieth time in three years.

I'm seething. Was that a joke that only entertains stupid people? Have they never heard of beans? Tofu? Tempeh? I wanna snap-twirl in all their faces; ain't nobody gonna talk to an herbivore like that.

But, whatever, let's talk about Oedipus. We all know the Oedipus story by now. He had no idea what he was doing was bad and will soon come back to bite him in the ass, but guess what: should've listened to the Oracles. That's Greek tragedy for ya – full stop, the end, moving on. I throw down my spoon into an empty BPA-free can of organic black bean soup, and I say, "I don't know why we still have to keep reading about Oedipus. You all already know how to act like motherfuckers."

For the first time in three years, all eyes on me.

After the words fly out of my mouth I realize I have to spend the next thirty weeks with these people. "I'm sorry. That was out of line. I'm sorry. Let's talk about tragedy."

When class ends, one of the playwrights pulls me aside: "What's going on? You're so serious now. You used to eat burgers and pizza all the time, and now you're carrying around containers of salad and cartons of soy milk and whatever else you have in your Mary Poppins Canvas Bag of Vegetarianism. It's weird, Dan. I get it – you're all excited about new foods. Congratulations, but it worries me. You meet some health guru in the desert and completely change your life? Dan, it makes me think you're susceptible to Scientology."

"*Excuse me?* First off: word choice, playwright. And, to set the record straight, eating healthy is in no way comparable to Scientology. Clear?"

"Okay, but it's weird. It's weird walking down the street with you. All of a sudden I'll go to say something, and you're gnawing on sheets of seaweed. You look like some hipster otter shoving sea vegetables into your beard. Look, we were all talking – we miss the old Dan, he was fun, he'd do shots of Jameson and say funny things. Look, we're all gonna meet up tonight and have drinks. You should come. Loosen up."

"I can't. I'm meeting up with a guy tonight, so..."

Why should I be the one to change? This reminds me of something Susan said in this morning's podcast. Other people won't appreciate the goals you make for yourself, because they want you to stay the same. As I build up strength and develop good habits, I'm fortifying myself. And I'm not going to compromise that for anyone.

• • •

But later that night I see this guy.

For once I think "he looks much better than his Grindr photo." He's got arms for days, stunningly attractive (he's got that little tricep indent goin' on!), but you also think, "if those arms wanted to, they could probably put me in the hospital."

"What's up? Can I get you a drink?" He grins.

I'm trying not to drink, but he has such a smooth voice... Yeah, I wanna get to know this guy —

"Jameson on the rocks!" I cheer.

The music is blaring, it's far too difficult to talk to him in this setting, but soon it doesn't matter because we are dancing, and I'm sipping more Irish whiskey, because I love it so. He's got one hand snapping a rhythm and another hand pulling me closer, and I feel his fingers on the small of my back, and I think, "I'm usually not into being the submissive one, but you made the first move, bro, and I am very curious to see where this goes."

Two Jamesons later, and it's hitting me harder than it's hit me before. We are making out on the dance floor. Sheila E. starts to play from the sound system, and I twirl around like I ain't never twirled before, because I do love me some Sheila. He pulls me in closer and says, "The moon up above shines down upon our skin," he whispers those lyrics into my ear, he's got this breathy grunt, and somehow I hear every nuance of his voice and feel every nuance of his hips... He seduces me into a slow dance to a fast song. That juxtaposition makes me swoon like 'damn, baby. You better than fish tacos.'

Before I know it we are stripping each other's clothes off back in his apartment on Avenue A; we cram ourselves into a bedroom way too small for our tall bodies.

I see his twin bed and wonder, "how does he fit in this?" He shoves me down on the bed, and I think, "whoa, this is happening." Ankles go places like they got secrets to tell me. He's got this nice chest, and he's pumping away, yes, baby, this *is* happening, go-go go-go *go!* This one moment comes when he kisses me on the lips, and our beards rub together... Neither of us can take anymore.

He pushes off of me and goes into the bathroom while I recover. I catch my breath. I go into the bathroom after him and sit down —

Why did I let him...

I go back to his room, he's got the light off, and he's curled up in bed. I try to lie next to him. He says, "My bed is really small. I mean, you can stay – if you want." And I do. He falls asleep, and I'm awake for a few hours, I watch one o'clock turn into three and four, and I try to fall asleep, too. Morning comes. I thought this morning I'd wake up in his arms.

But he's curled into a ball on one side. I see he has his underwear on, and I'm still naked. I find my boxer-briefs, put them on as I watch him in his flannel sheet bed, holding a pillow like I'd want him to hold me. He's drooled a bit, and I wish I'd woken up with drool on my neck. I have on my underwear, my pants; I stretch into my shirt and stand on one leg to put on each sock. I watch him as I do this. I watch him as he sleeps. And then I put

DAN BERNITT

my shoes on and sneak out and slip into a diner on 7th and A. I tie my laces as I look at the menu, the sunrise on this Saturday morning shining inside.

I sit at the counter by myself and make a list of all the menu items I can't eat. Bacon, sausage, and I'm trying to be vegan, so I also can't have eggs. The pancakes probably have some kind of dairy. The waitress looks at me expectantly. I ask, "Do you all have anything that's vegan?"

She folds her arms and glares. "We got juice. Coffee. You want toast? No butter, right. Jelly? Ooh, Mister Fancy. Alright, comin' right up."

Luckily it's too early for couples to brunch together. It's probably best that guy isn't here, because this would be... Anyway. The waitress comes back with my order. "I made sure we didn't put bacon fat on yer toast. Enjoy, kiddo."

I bite into the toast. Even with jelly it's impossibly dry to eat. I sip coffee that's bitter because it's been on the burner for too long. And the juice? It's Sunny Delight. So I drink water on this Saturday morning as the sun shines into the diner.

• • •

A month later I'm in the emergency room at Beth Israel, and I – don't know what's going on. I've got needles in my arms, I'd slept for three days, I don't know the last time I had a meal. I can barely speak because my tonsils have swelled so much they hug. My face is white as cauliflower, and I do not feel pretty.

It'd been an illness that gradually got worse. I looked up all the ways I could try to make myself better naturally: wheatgrass juice, onion juice, garlic soup. This has done nothing except stink up my apartment. But I don't even understand why any of this is happening because I've been eating so healthy recently. I'm a full-fledged vegan now. Why am I not in pristine health? Here I am in the hospital where they tell me, "You're very sick. We don't know what's wrong with you, but we have a few questions and tests."

I'm unable to swallow my own saliva. I nod my head to answer.

"Have you slept with anyone recently? Was it with a guy? Did you or he wear condoms? Did you give or —"

"Received," I choke out.

"We should do an HIV test. You might be seroconverting. Your symptoms are very similar to the early stages of infection. You also need food, because you say you haven't eaten in three days."

She vanishes behind the curtain, and I am alone in this curtained cell.

Oh, my God.

What if I have HIV?

This is going to limit my future in so many ways.

While the nurse is gone, I pull out my phone, and I think of calling my mother, but this also something I feel like I cannot talk to her about: I'm scared to tell my mother that I'm an atheist and that I'm a sexually-active gay man. She knows I'm sick, I let her know that, but she doesn't know why. And I don't know why either. Yet. But I pull out my phone, and I start to research "natural treatments for HIV."

The nurse returns with a swab, and I scratch up the inside of my mouth as she sets down food in front of me. And then she takes the swab and *leaves*! What? You're leaving? I've had a few HIV tests done in my life, and usually I get to sit with a nice person who asks questions like, "will you kill yourself if you find out you're positive?" Not today.

And then I look down at the cellophane-wrapped sandwiches. Chicken salad on wheat bread; egg salad on white. As I sip on the apple juice she left,

I think about what I've heard about plastics, how they leak chemicals onto food, how they might cause cancer. Now that I'm vegan I can't eat any of this, even if I could swallow. I want to ask if someone could go to a smoothie place and get me a drink with spinach and kale and maybe some goji berries. But no, I get to sit here with *this* food—food that doesn't heal!—and my worrying brain.

There were some painkillers in the IV, so it's easier to swallow the apple juice. But I'm only taking small sips, because I don't know if this is fresh, I don't know if this is not from concentrate, it might have some added sugars. I dwell on the origins of the juice to distract myself from the fact I might have HIV.

The nurse comes back: "Why haven't you eaten anything?! Do I have to stand here until you eat?"

I look at the nurse. I look at the sandwiches. I'm afraid. I don't know how this food will make me feel. I don't want to risk getting sicker. I open the chicken sandwich and pick at the wheat bread.

She looks at me as I take these tiny bites.

"Your test came back negative."

Thank God.

"But you might have mono."

The kissing disease?! I thought only tenth-graders got that.

"You have to take it easy for the next two weeks. And, honey, you're still infectious, so you can't really kiss anyone for up to a year."

What?! A year? I'm a 24-year-old gay man, living in New York City's East Village: the gayborhood. And now I can't even *kiss* anyone?

So, Officer, just to recap: I was so lonely living in the desert for three months, and the only person I had to talk to was a 1990s infomercial personality. I came back to New York and felt alienated by the people I used to hang out with, and now the people I want to hang out with *and kiss on the mouth* are off-limits. How could this possibly get worse?!

The nurse says, "Well, I guess you have an excuse to go home and watch Netflix. Be sure to eat something when you get home. Here, take this sandwich."

Once I'm outside I throw away that toxic crap and walk home. I text my mother: "Next two weeks off. I have mono."

"Oh no, baby!!!" (Triple exclamation point.) "Do u need anything? I'll put $ in u r bank account."

"Thanks, Mom."

A little while later, she texts: "I'm on Google. Lots of ways 2 get mono. Maybe someone sneezed? NYC is a big C!"

I text back: "Pretty sure I got it from making out with a guy."

Radio silence for several blocks. I'm walking up four flights of stairs to my apartment when she texts back: "It's always fun to make memories."

• • •

I immediately start watching Netflix. The first thing I watch is a documentary about food. In the opening credits it proclaims, "Let thy food be thy medicine!" I learn that if people would stop eating meat and dairy and sugar, they'd be healed of all their ailments. There's this doctor — he may not be an MD, but he has a PhD — he says that we can heal people with the right doses of vitamins. Yeah, vitamins! He's healed people suffering from all kinds of ailments: Alzheimer's, cancer, debilitating depression. But then some MD stepped in, as the medicine boys do, and said all those vitamins might be dangerous. What does *he* know?!

That documentary made me so mad, and then I watched one about how we import our fruits and vegetables from all over the world. Did you know that when the food arrives here, it's already begun to rot? *Ew!* But wait, have you heard the dangers of cooking your food? Heat makes food develop carcinogens. I don't know about you, but I don't want to eat plates of cancer. I don't wanna eat rotting food. I sit on my couch with swollen tonsils and resolve: when I can eat again, I will eat fresh, local things. Only.

I exhaust the supply of food documentaries and graduate to the ones about the entire world. Like, what's happening to the ozone? What's happening to the endangered species? I watch another documentary about the environment and how our food supply affects it. I learn about these things called monocultures; they are these giant fields where only one crop grows. Giant fields of wheat, corn, soybeans, all covered with pesticides. The crops aren't being rotated, so the nutrients in the soil are vanishing, so without healthy topsoil... Well, just wait 'til the monoculture brings the dust bowl back to America.

Then I saw stuff about corporations. And then on YouTube I learned about chemtrails and the Illuminati and the Reptilian Elite lizard people!

I realize maybe I should take a break from the Internet, but then I found out something even scarier that won't let me take a break. It starts with M. And, no, it's bigger than Monsanto.

Answer: Mathematics.

Now, I love math. I love numbers. But I saw this video on YouTube called "The Most Important Video You'll Ever See. Parts 1-8." Stay with me.

The video talked about doubling time. Whenever you find a rate of growth, and you want to know how long it'll take for something to double, divide 70% by that growth rate. Let's say you have $1,000 invested, and it returns 7% each year. 70% divided by 7% is ten. So, in ten years, you'll have twice what you put in: you'll have $2,000 invested. In another ten years, $4,000, and so forth, exponentially.

That's pretty cool, but let's apply this to something else. Let's say oil consumption is rising at an annual rate of 7%. What does that mean? In ten years, we will be using twice the oil we're using now.

Now, luckily oil consumption is not rising at a rate of *seven* percent. But it is rising. So it's just a matter of time.

Oil is used for nearly everything: plastics, gas, electricity, pesticides... If we don't have oil, we're

DAN BERNITT

screwed. Since oil isn't renewable, our oil reserves continue to dwindle, while at the same time our world population is rising. Our world population is rising at a rate that will leave us with 14 billion people in less than sixty years. Fourteen billion by 2070. Oil might run out before then, because if global warming doesn't kill us off first, we will need more energy and food to take care of all of us. Should we all just die and stop using our resources?! Should we kill all the babies?

Don't be quiet! The answer is no. No! That's crazy. No. But the math...

I slam shut my computer. It was under a nurse's orders that I watch Netflix. Two weeks of watching stuff on the Internet was not a vacation. I don't know what other people watch on Netflix, but I try to keep it educational. This is scaring me so much I want to find religion. Heaven is infinitely huge and doesn't need oil, but I'm not gonna start reading fairy tales as fact. How do we live in this world?

All this makes me want to live off the land, but how will I feed myself until the harvest comes? And what do I mean by "harvest?" I've never had a garden. The only plant I ever had I killed, and it was a fucking Christmas cactus.

Netflix used to describe things I liked as "deadpan TV comedies" and "quirky independent movies." I've tried forgetting about all this, but I've watched so many that now all it will only recommend more "topical traumas" and "doomsday documentaries."

• • •

When I go back to class after my recovery, I feel like a zombie. This planet wants to shake us off. I'm not much help to my classmates either. If my mind ever wanders, I start thinking about how big the Universe is and how fragile our world is. And when I do pay attention, I think things like, "Why is your play set in New York City? Are you trying to write a history play? It's gonna be underwater in twenty years."

I can't get out of this way of thinking.

My classmates are very generous. They ask me what's going on, and I say, "I—I just *can't* anymore." To cheer me up, they all offer to go to a vegan restaurant with me. They show me how much they're enjoying themselves as they eat grilled marinated tofu and tempeh reubens. Afterwards Mr. Sugar Crash pulls me aside and says, "Yeah, man, you were right. I feel a lot better now. Thanks, bud."

This is really sweet, but I still feel like I'm not doing enough. I can always eat cleaner. Spring break arrives, and I decide to make my final transformation: raw foods only.

I finish off a mason jar of homemade soy milk and toss out my grains. Only raw fruits and vegetables from here on. My final transformation. I make a grocery list – strawberries, *un*roasted sunflower seeds, grapes, bananas, whatever else I can find.

I pop in my earbuds and cue up a Susan Powter podcast. In the latest one, Susan scolds *The New York Times* for publishing an article about a possible "fat gene."

"You would not believe, you would not believe, *The New York Times*. A fat gene? There is nothing genetic. Let me read, I quote: 'The subjects of a study about weight loss were put on a strict diet of 550 calories per day.' This is not genetics. This is starvation, people! What ethical doctor doesn't know this?! Of course these people aren't going to lose weight. The body wants to survive, but these poor people are having their metabolism destroyed."

She continues on for a half-hour, ripping apart the article sentence by sentence, and peppering in the E-word — ethical.

"Whatever. *The New York Times* is full of shit, it's irresponsible, anyone who believes there's a 'fat gene' is an idiot. I encourage everyone listening, please, *please*, people, do me a favor: write this sorry woman writer and let her know the truth."

While I walk and listen, I think, "Susan's very thorough with this. This sounds like some seriously bad journalism." I look up the author's email address and send her a message with a link to the podcast: "This might be worth a listen."

I've gone two days on this raw diet so far, I'm at the detox stage, I went cold turkey on coffee because even hot water is verboten, but I'll get through it and feel incredible.

When I reach Whole Foods, I decide my first meal will be seedless grapes and strawberries. Once they're in my basket, I think, "whoa, wait. This single meal is going to cost me about ten bucks." Vegetables are a little cheaper, but how am I going to be full with this stuff?

But then I remember one raw foodist blog I read. This guy eats fifteen bananas a day. What is this going to cost me, so I weigh them — seven dollars and twenty-six cents. For fifteen bananas. Per day.

For the rest of my life. I don't have that kind of money. That's crazy.

"Who the hell has money to be a raw foodist?"

I find that I'm not just thinking this; I'm starting to say it out loud in the produce department.

"Excuse me, who's able to afford any of this? I've thought about getting a Costco membership, but I don't want industrial fruit, and while it'd be good exercise I don't want to carry home fifteen bananas every day. Plus strawberries and grapes and mangoes and kiwi and seeds and — Is it even possible to be a raw foodist in this world? I was told I could be anything I wanted to be, but I can't even be a raw foodist. And, people, this food, by being here, is already starting to rot. Didja know that? We can't get local bananas in New York. How are we gonna get food when the bee colonies collapse? Pesticides are killing off everything. What about the topsoil? What about when all those nutrients are gone? What about the end of oil, bananas can't come to the mainland from Hawaii, we should all move to Hawaii, but it's expensive and the mail is real slow, but at least we'd have all the bananas all the time, but no, nope, not gonna happen because now all we have left to do is starve and die *or* be in this stupid city and spend *thirty dollars a day* on fresh fruit. This is the only way to be healthy, people; I looked it up! I want to be an enlightened eater, but I don't have $11,000 a year to spend on bananas. What do you think I am, Whole Foods; what do you think I am, America; what do you think I am, banana rack?! The only people who pay for enlightenment are Scientologists, and I am not, I repeat, I am not a Scientologist, clear?"

My phone buzzes in my pocket. What fresh hell is this? It's an email from the writer at the *Times*. "Thanks for getting in touch, but given the title of the podcast, I think I'll pass."

Okay, so I know the title of the podcast was "Fuck you, *New York Times*," but she doesn't want to hear a critique? "Well, *fine!*"

As I say that, I watch the bananas in my hand leave my hand and sail over the produce department. Like a discus. My hand clenches shut, trying to grab them back, but it's far too late because they're flying, they're flying high, they're going faster, and I pray, "please, bananas, land in someone's basket."

Nope. They hit the meat department case and tumble onto the floor. Two guys working look at me. One shouts, "Dude. What the hell?" His buddy walks over to a phone and starts dialing, "I think we have a homeless guy throwing stuff?"

I rush over to the bananas, now battered and bruised, and scramble to the front of the store to check out. I'm with the cashier, and she's checking me out, and I see over my shoulder the guy from the meat department running toward me, shouting, "hey buddy!" The cashier weighs my fifteen bananas, and I look in my wallet, and I don't have any cash on me, and I don't want to answer to Mr. Meat Guy, so I just grab the sack of grapes, and I slam down my debit card and say, "Here, just charge me." And I sprint out of the store, holding the grapes like a football, and run as fast as I can.

I reach Third Avenue and slow down. My hamstrings are killing me. I'm hungry, so I start eating the grapes and muttering to myself on the sidewalk.

"Oh, no. I can't go back there. Luckily there's another Whole Foods. Ugh, but I left my card there. It has my name on it. Dan! Well, I could just call my bank and cancel it."

When I look at my phone, my rage boils over again – the writer at the *Times*! No one gets away with being wrong. I shove more grapes into my mouth as I think through ways to annihilate her. I will be vindicated. I start reading her article; yep, just like Susan said.

But then – that's funny – at the bottom of the page, there's a link. Several links. Susan didn't say this article had seven more pages. That's – that's a strange omission. But she read this. Right?

Did she *not* read this?

She didn't even read this! If she's wrong about this, what else might she be wrong about?

What am *I* wrong about?

I might be wrong about everything...

Oh, no, I can't be wrong. I wouldn't be wrong about this. This came from the earth! This is true.

But wait. Am I wrong? I might be wrong about everything. Oh, *no*.

What have I done? What have I been doing?

I see my reflection in a storefront, and I think, "Oh, my God, that's me. That's me spitting out grapes onto the sidewalk of Third Avenue." My beard's bushier than it's ever been. My hair's growing out, and the way it's starting to thin doesn't look appealing at all. I look at myself. I look at myself, and I look. Wow, all that led to this. This is what I've turned into...

So, I walked home. I buzzed my head. I trimmed my beard. I put on a clean shirt, that's why I look different. I wanted to look sane when I came back to this Whole Foods.

Officer, like I said, it's really difficult to explain. It's a culmination of a lot of things. What I did was wrong: I shouldn't have run out of here with a sack of grapes.

You might be sitting in judgment. You might be thinking I'm ridiculous. In telling you this, I'm realizing now that, I don't know, maybe I need to get help?

I just want to know I'm not alone.

But I —

I snapped.

There's so much that's terrifying happening in the world, and how are we supposed to deal with it?

I promise: No more Netflix. No more podcasts. I wrote back to the writer at the *Times*, and I said, "I am so sorry. I'm embarrassed. I stopped thinking."

I feel betrayed, all this seemed so true — and some of it still might be true.

I don't know what's true anymore.

And I don't know how to act.

But I don't have a record; I'm not dangerous; I will be better behaved. Give me a warning, we don't need to press charges, like...

Please. I'm sorry.

Can we move forward?

Can we move on? I'll pay for everything.

I just want my card back.

I want my friends back.

I want to eat.

I want to eat *with people* again.

Like a normal person.

This Is
Stonewall

WHEN I CAME OUT OF THE CLOSET AT THE age of 14, my parents were very supportive. "We just want you to be happy, honey."

When I broke up with my first boyfriend at 15, they decided I shouldn't date anymore. "We just don't want you to get hurt, honey," they told me. They didn't specify if that meant emotionally or physically, and I was too flabbergasted to ask for a clarification.

A month later I started a secret relationship, and when he dumped me to spend more time doing yoga, my high school broken-hearted self was too scared to tell my parents why I was suddenly so sad all the time. I didn't want to get in trouble.

If I can't actively *be* gay, then I'll live vicariously through the stories of people who can. I checked out all the books on homosexuality the Lexington Public Library had, and I took myself on dates with books until I moved into college.

I met Randy when I turned 22, eight years after I came out of the closet. It's been eight years, and even though I had boyfriends during college, I'm still figuring out how to date.

A mutual friend connected us when he found out I was moving to New York for graduate school. Randy and I made plans to meet up soon after I arrived. We meet at Astor Place. I get off the 6 train and meet him on the corner of Starbucks and Starbucks. He pushes back his curly hair, smiles, and says he's hungry. We walk east, toward Alphabet City, towards Avenues A and B and C and D and dart into a Chipotle on St. Marks. Together we eat, we shovel rice and beans and guacamole and corn into our mouths. We exchange underhanded jokes, jokes aimed to make the other laugh, jokes that try to test waters before we enter them. He laughs, I laugh, I'm learning how to flirt.

We walk further east, past First Avenue toward A onto Tompkins Square Park. We look at the dogs in the dog park and start to make up stories about the hierarchy among the larger dogs. We leave, and he throws away his Chipotle cup. He reads the sign over the trash can: "This is your park / Please / Keep it clean." He keeps saying "This is your park please" over and over and over until I laugh and laugh and laugh.

We walk south, south toward rice pudding. Lost, we don't know which way to go. Lost, we try to find ways to the pudding place: Rice to Riches, Rice to Riches, I know it was on Prince Street, I say. Or maybe it was Spring. At an intersection he pushes back his hair, widens his eyes. "Where are we?" He asks. A few more blocks; if we can't find it, we'll go somewhere else, okay?

Two blocks later we stumble inside – our mouths water at the flavors, the cinnamon raisin, the chai latte, the chocolate torte. We order a single serving of the cinnamon raisin with two spoons. Across from each other at a freestanding table, we spoon the pudding into our mouths. He says: "This is your rice pudding please" as he feeds me a spoonful. We empty the dish, then exit back onto the street.

On Spring Street, walking west toward Lafayette, I put my hand in his briefly – long enough to ask "Where do you wanna go?" The sun begins to set behind the buildings of downtown, also heading west. We walk toward the sunset to Washington Square Park. We arrive and find a patch of grass to rest on. He lies down and stretches out his arms for me to lie down with him.

I pretend to stretch and take a glance around me,

checking out the types of people, sizing them up.

"Come here," he says.

I lie down with him, resting my head against his chest, on top of his heart, quietly thumping there. He puts his arm around me, holding me close. I tilt my head up to see the darkening sky.

We rest there. We lie there with our silence and the murmur of people playing frisbee, the shuffling of bags, the rumble of the street around us. He plays with my hair, and I look up briefly - and we kiss. He kisses me on the lips, gently biting my bottom lip.

And I pull away.

"I'm really, really sorry. It's just - I don't know how to do this."

He smiles. "It's okay."

"So, where do you wanna go now? We could head back uptown, back up to my apartment in Harlem."

Smiling, he says sure.

We walk north, west, east, south, all over looking for the D train. "Um, where are we?" He asks as we turn onto West Fourth Street. "I know there's a D train stop on West Fourth, we'll just walk until we see it." We walk further and further, no trains; we intersect with Christopher Street.

I look around and think, "Oh, my goodness, this is Christopher Street." I pull Randy down the street, and I point out all these places I've read about when learning my own queer history. On the corner of Christopher and Gay streets is the site of the Oscar Wilde Bookstore, one of the oldest gay bookstores in America, one of the only places where gay people could find themselves in stories. We walk further, and just before Seventh Avenue, I find myself standing in front of The Stonewall Inn.

"Randy, this is Stonewall."

"What's that?" He asks.

"You don't know what Stonewall is?! Oh, my God! June 28, 1969, people started rioting against the police because they were tired of having their lives destroyed, tired of being arrested for petty and frivolous things, tired of being targeted because they were gay, and they fought back, they weren't gonna take it anymore! These are the streets where the gay rights movement started, these are the streets where drag queens ripped up parking meters from the ground and chased away the police! This is our mythology, Randy! How can you be a young gay man in America and not know what Stonewall is?!"

And he answers: "How do you not know how to hold my hand?"

Touché.

"You're right. I'm sorry. I'm sorry I'm so hesitant to hold your hand; it's just something I need to get used to." He offers his hand. And I take it. We walk together away from the Stonewall, up Seventh Avenue. After we walk away from all things rainbow, I give his hand a squeeze and drop it.

We walk to a subway station and ride the train uptown together. He asks: "Where are we?"

"A subway car?"

"No, I mean, where are *we*?"

I look at him, and I say, "I don't know, but – I've enjoyed our night so far. Maybe we can see where it goes?"

As the train runs express from 59th Street to my apartment in Harlem, he puts his arm along the top of the seat, around my shoulders. "You're okay," he whispers in my ear. I rest my head on his shoulder. An older Latin woman sits across from us, and she smiles. I shut my eyes as the subway car speeds under the city streets, rocking us in the tunnel, a gentle sway from side to side.

Ghoti

HOW DO YOU PRONOUNCE THESE WORDS?

tough   women   situation   ghoti

That last one tends to trip up people. Let's get on the same page. How do you pronounce the underlined portion of each word?

tou**gh**   w**o**men   situa**ti**on

gh   **o**   **ti**

ghoti

No wonder it's difficult for speakers of other languages to grasp all the English pronunciation rules. With all the idiosyncracies, it's almost like English is a foreign language to itself. (This spelling is usually attributed to George Bernard Shaw. There's also a fun respelling of the word potato: ghoughpteighbteau. For now, let's look at ghoti.)

Ghoti. Fish. Ghoti. Ghoti. Fish. Fish. Ghoti. Ghoti. Ghoti. Fish. Fish. Fish. Ghoti. Ghoti. Fish. Fish. Ghoti. In your community. In your city. Ghoti. Fish. Ghoti. Fish. Ghoti. Do you understand?

These are the words spoken by a man who looks like a sixtysomething pirate chef. We're on a boat. I met him last night when I arrived in Venice, Italy, for a weeklong vacation with my dear friend Shayla Lawson. Because the middle of March has unpredictable weather, Shayla's many flights were delayed or canceled. We had to purchase an entirely different itinerary—anyway, long, expensive story aside, I arrived a day before her. I arrived a day before my guide, in a place she's raved about for the past eight years, in a place where I don't know anyone, the language, or where we're staying. Luckily while I crossed the Atlantic overnight, Shayla contacted her friends in Venice, and one offered to show me around once I landed.

Clair is a short redheaded Irish woman who, after a spritz and carafe and a half of wine, proves she can drink me under any table. I also learn very quickly that Dubliners and American Southerners do not share the same set of manners. We stop by a restaurant for a drink and asked a busy waitress to stop by our table when she had a free moment. Twenty minutes later, the waitress turns over a sign in the window that says they're closed.

Of course, our friend Clair storms inside.

"We wanted to order food. You *forgot* about us."

I follow her, embarrassed by the situation, but it looks like the staff are more embarrassed than I am. The chef fans away the conflict: "Clams or shellfish?" Clair says clams. I say shellfish like a reflex. And then he pours us a full carafe of red wine.

"Go sit."

Wow, what generosity.

"Excuse me," Clair says. And I think, "Good God, what else now?" She looks to the other side of the room and points at a small stage. "You have live music here?"

The chef nods.

"My friend here plays music. He's visiting from New York. He and his friend have an act."

We do?

And I think, okay, so ten years ago Shayla and I did a performance at the Kentucky Women Writers Conference. It was at a dinner for the author of *Sex & The City*. After some real-life Carrie Bradshaw blew smoke in my face, Shayla and I did acoustic folk versions of rap and Beyoncé. It was a fun party trick, but let's not kid ourselves. I play guitar, and while I wanted to be a folksinger like Ani DiFranco, sometimes things happen—things happen, and you put your dreams on hold. I wouldn't necessarily identify as a musician, but I do enjoy playing the guitar.

The restaurant staff suddenly takes an interest in the bald, bearded, New York musician standing in front of them. And then I realize that that person they're looking at is tall, scruffy writer me.

"What kind of music do you play?"

I try to answer with something that might disinterest them: "American folk."

There's a redheaded server with a red beard who reminds me of a brawny version of my ex-boyfriend. His eyes light up, just like Cameron's eyes would light up when he saw me. "I *love* American folk." The chef says something to the redhead, who then asks, "He wants to know if you all can play tomorrow afternoon."

"They sure can!" Clair buts into the conversation, and apparently she's now my agent. "And Shayla's on her flight right now!"

I pull her aside. "Clair. I don't have a guitar."

"Don't worry! You'll find one."

I don't remember much of what happened next.

It exists in snippets:

they refused to let us pay for our meal;

the chef of the restaurant commented about my eyes, he said I had "artist eyes" or the eyes of a "genuine artist" or a "true artist" or something;

I started to get a little anxious about what other people see in me, the things I will never see for myself, and then I downed several glasses of prosecco to forget that thought;

I text the crush I have who also happens to be a bassist and tell him I have a gig and maybe he should fly over to play and "btdubs I love you;"

I text Shayla and tell her to start memorizing songs because "we've just turned into a sensation;"

I enjoy more red wine as I tell a stranger the story as it unfolds. "I've been here for seven hours, and this is happening." She says, "I've been here for seven years, and it's completely changed my life!"

"That's great!" I slur. "But I still have to find a guitar for my gig tomorrow afternoon!"

I wake up in the morning—guitarless and with such a headache. I'm here on vacation, and I'm not relaxing. Last night I got a music gig without playing a single note, because someone *said* I'm a musician. Someone else looked in my eyes and thought, "That guy's an artist. I'm gonna give him lots to eat and even more to drink." What does any of this mean?

I can't go back to that restaurant without Shayla because I don't want to feel the embarrassment of not reciprocating. I don't even want to go outside because I'm afraid I'll run into the chef. I'm afraid he'll ask me to play *right now*. I'm afraid he'll see my eyes again; I'm afraid the look he saw of genuine artistry has been replaced with blood-red terror.

Shayla arrives at 3:00, and we rush over to the restaurant. When the chef sees me, his eyes lock on me. He smiles and claps a hand on my shoulder. "You're here."

Shayla begins apologizing—in Italian. The chef fans away the apology and pours us wine. He offers us chicetti, little slices of bread topped with meats and cheeses and roasted vegetables. We eat. We offer to pay, but he shakes his head.

"No. You will come back Sunday, and you will play. Come with me." Outside the restaurant, he shows us his motorboat, the only way to transport oneself through Venice's web of canals.

"Come."

He takes us on a tour.

As Shayla and I balance on the boat, Maurizio navigates us around, and my mind calms.

We serpentine between buildings, then we speed into the Grand Canal. He encourages us to echo our voices under the Rialto Bridge.

"Hoy!" We call.

Hoy!

We grin, blissful. Lucky.

But I'm still freaking out. Now we have a gig on Sunday. We still have to get me an instrument and learn songs again. We have to learn what it's like to perform together after not doing a gig in ten years. We have to get the band back together!

Venice is gorgeous. I want to keep shouting under the Rialto Bridge. I want to walk gingerly along all the canals (perhaps holding hands with that redhead), but there's no time to relax. There is no time for handholding.

It's Friday. It's too late in the day now to find a guitar shop, so we wake up early Saturday to do a search. We walk the streets and see vendors with fruit stands, we pass windows with crisply tailored suits, we see restaurants with outdoor seating, couples and families enjoying a cool morning. We pass windows with brightly colored shoes, pizza slices ready to reheat, gelato with its globs of fruit, drizzles of chocolate, mounds of whipped cream on top... the many things Venice offers are such sweet distractions. But when I see a trash can with a fish on it, I realize we have yet to pass a guitar shop. We looked up where one might be, but there's no clear way to arrive at any destination. Getting lost is the Venetian way.

With the clock ticking closer to siesta, when all the shops close for the afternoon, our chances of finding a guitar grow closer to nil. I can't go back to this man *again* and tell him, "sorry, I can't do a gig, thanks for taking me out on your boat and giving me a free meal and lots of wine and introducing me to your community." The least I can do is find a guitar in a city I've never been to and play some songs I just learned. That should be the easy part, right?

We pass more restaurants and gelato and cross bridges over gondolas and more restaurants and gelato and *how come we haven't found a guitar shop* and more bridges and restaurants and gelato and bridges and bridges and gelato and shoes and pizza and gelato and restaurants and restaurants and a grocery store and a wine shop and it's ten minutes before siesta and bridges and restaurants and bridges and *oh my god there's a guitar shop*.

In the center of the window I see an acoustic-electric traveler-sized guitar. This guitar will plug into the restaurant's sound system. This guitar will fit in the overhead bin on my flight back to America. This guitar costs 240 Euro. I hadn't planned for any of this. I don't know if it's worth it.

#yolo — I have a guitar.

Msg(1/2) USAA ALERT:
Please verify Credit Card
Charges for your card
ending in 8276:
Date: 15Mar
Amt: $334.**
Where: ZAGGIA
STRUMENTI MUSIC IT
Are any

Msg(2/2) of these
transactions fraud? Reply
Y or N.
To stop receiving Credit
Card fraud alerts reply
STOP.

Text Message   Send

My bank immediately sends me a text message.

No, this is not fraud. This is opportunity.

Shayla and I sit in a small square surrounded by buildings and begin to sing. As we perform, our separate elements of voice and strums lean against each other. We're symbiotic again. On occasion she leads with singing, and other times I lead with chords. People pass, a few take photos of us (what?), and then we grab lunch and make our setlist: Frank Ocean, Lady Gaga, Prince, Miley Cyrus, Marvin Gaye, and I now realize all those nights in high school that I invested in teaching myself how to play guitar by using tabulature for dozens of Ani DiFranco songs has finally had some kind of return.

It's been years since I played for any extended period of time, but the muscle memory is there. We rehearse so much in one day that the next morning, after dreaming what our performance will be like, I wake up with blisters on my fingers.

I can still play, though I'm now tender, and we head over to the restaurant. The place is busy, and the wait staff rush to set up for the crowd of a hundred-plus who show each Sunday. We are shown the stage and a crate of audio cables and the four-channel audio mixer, and people are filing in to eat as we plug in microphones and check sound.

My guitar doesn't come through the system, and I don't know if it's the cable or the guitar, did I buy a dud?, and then the audience looks at us like we are there to entertain, and we've yet to do a sound check, maybe we will get out some songs, so we play a bit, and the sound feeds back, and I start to think, *oh no, how embarrassing is this? Do these Italians see two flunkies who don't know what they're doing?* I use a microphone to pick up sound from my guitar, but the levels are all off, and I can't hear myself, and people are in various stages of paying attention or covering their ears when the sound feeds back *again*, and Shayla can't hear me because we don't have any monitors, and we troubleshoot onstage in front of this brunch crowd of faces I cannot read: do they pity us, do they want to hear us, do they want to eat and get out, what?

As I begin to doubt my audience, I begin to doubt myself.

I remember back when I was in high school, and I wanted to be a folksinger. I wanted to write songs and perform and travel, and there was this one guy in my biology class, this guy in my biology class who *smelled* like fish, people would joke behind his back and call him Fish Boy or Fishie or something else cruel. I felt bad for him. He found out I played music, and he was curious about the songs I wrote, and we chatted on AOL Instant Messenger, and he told me that he enjoyed my songwriting, and he was one of the first people to take an interest in my work. And then one day it shifted, he shifted, he told me that nothing was good, nothing was ever good, he had been lying to me all along.

I think about the lie, and back in real life, back in the Venetian restaurant, I see a man gesture strumming a guitar, and he gives me a thumbs up. Here's an encouraging stranger, and I still have this jerk from high school stuck in my head. I think about how when I was told the lie, suddenly my life theme of betrayal trauma resurfaces, and—the guy in high school told me he and his dad, his dad who I met, his dad who encouraged me in writing, he tells me they listened to my songs, and together they turned me into a punching bag and laughed about the things I couldn't do. "You can't sing. You can't play. You're not good. We'd been lying to you all along. We didn't have the heart to tell you."

I don't know what it was that now made him have the heart to tell me. I don't know what makes people so benevolent. Or is it malevolent?

And here I am in Venice, onstage for a brunch crowd, and Jerkface now sits in my head. It's taken him twelve or thirteen years to make a return journey, like a comet in space that comes back every so often. He's like a comet that makes a select group of people go crazy and believe that if only they kill themselves they'll finally reach their salvation.

What scares me is I may be one of those people who's willing to destroy himself in desperation for salvation.

Yes, it's in the past. Yes, it's behind me. But why is it now right in front of me while I'm on vacation—*in Venice?!*

As I strum on my guitar, testing the sound, I think, "why not take the risk? Will it really matter if I fail? Will I ever see these people again?"

Maybe! It could be terrifying.

But then another voice enters my head: an instructor I had in graduate school. "Dan, you have the capacity to be so much better than you are. So dare to fail." Only a few months after he said this, he had a stroke, rendering him unable to teach, and a few months after that he died.

Am I really going to let some high school chump

hold me back with some crap he and his dad said to me twelve years ago? *Yeah!* Yes.

God, that sounds so stupid.

No. Nancy Reagan taught me that word for a reason. I learned Ani DiFranco's songs for a reason. Shayla's singing her heart out. I could at least dare to do something. I will slap this guitar. I will jam out. I will fingerpick these strings, and, dammit, maybe I'm gonna sing!

Because I will not let Arthur Storch's commandment go unfollowed. I will not let down Shayla Lawson. I will not waste the energy and money and time and attention that people, organizations, schools, and festivals have invested in me. I call forth these demons and say, "To hell with you." I call forth Arthur and Shayla and every summary of a hero's journey because I'm feeling it now!

I call forth Tim and Fred and Trish and Tonya and Herman and Ani and Kelly and Ellen and David and Mitchell and Nikky and Eugene O'Neill and Frank and Chris and Christopher and Ron and even the artist we now know as Prince.

Blisters be damned, I will not go down easy.

In closing, people clapped, people shook our hands, some people danced. One lady even choked up at a Miley Cyrus cover. We were invited to do gigs in two more restaurants. We got paid in wine and beef carpaccio and fifty Euros each. We ate fish and pasta covered with basil and freshly grated asiago.

As Shayla and I ate our fish (fish, fish...), I took a moment before another bite to look outside myself, to look in again, to encourage:

may you pull the juicy meat from the bones;

may you sit with the ones you so deeply admire,
in settings that live up to
the fairy tale expectations;

may you finally dismiss anyone
who has taken up residence in your head;

may you be able to say to them:
"you do not sit with me now."

Beneath all bitterness and negativity and jealousy and vitriol, they can only dream of having what you have. They can only dream of having *this*.

This. This. This. This. This. This. This.

In your community. In your city.

This. This. This. *This*. Do you understand?

DAN BERNITT is an American author, playwright, and performer. His solo performances include *Yelling at Bananas in Whole Foods* (2013); *Phi Alpha Gamma* (2008); *Thanks for the Scabies, Jerkface!* (2006); *The Gayer Show* (with Les Kurkendaal, 2009); and *Moments of Disconnect* (2004); and they have been featured in venues internationally, from Minneapolis and Cape Cod to New York and Dublin. He has received numerous grants and fellowships from arts organizations, including an Al Smith Fellowship in Playwriting from the Kentucky Arts Council. A recipient of the Robert Chesley Award for Lesbian and Gay Playwriting, his books of plays, *Dose: Plays & Monologues* and *Phi Alpha Gamma*, were named finalists for the Lambda Literary Award.

www.danbernitt.com